Tips for Reading Together

Children learn best when reading is fun.

- Talk about the title and the pictures on the cover.
- Discuss what you think the story might be about.
- Read the story together, inviting your child to read as much of it as they can.
- Give lots of praise as your child reads, and help them when necessary.
- Try different ways of helping if they get stuck on a word. For example, get them to say the first sound of the word, or break it into chunks, or read the whole sentence again, trying to guess the word. Focus on the meaning.
- Have fun finding the hidden letters.
- Re-read the story later, encouraging your child to read as much of it as they can.

Children enjoy re-reading stories and this helps to build their confidence.

Have fun!

Find the letters and letter shapes hidden in the pictures that spell out the words SHRINKING POWDER.

Shrinking Powder

Written by Roderick Hunt
Illustrated by Alex Brychta

OXFORD
UNIVERSITY PRESS

Dad did the washing, but he put
the clothes in a hot wash.

"Oh no!" said Dad. "The clothes have shrunk."

"Look at my top," said Kipper.

"Look at my jeans," said Biff.

"Sorry," said Dad. "I forgot to set the washing machine. It was too hot."

Chip made a little boy with the clothes that had shrunk.

"That's a good joke," laughed Biff.

Suddenly, the magic key began to glow. It took the children into an adventure.

The key took them to a shop.
It sold magic tricks and strange
things.

"Wow!" said Chip. "It's a joke
shop. But there's nobody here.
I think the shop is shut."

Suddenly, there was a loud POP
and a puff of purple smoke.
"What's that?" asked Chip.

A boy was standing in the shop.
"I'm sorry about all the smoke,"
he said.

"I'm Jake," said the boy. "I'm learning to be a wizard. Watch this."

"Hooray! It works," said Jake,
"but learning to be a wizard is not
easy."

Jake took a tin out of his pocket.
"I want to try this," he said.

"It's shrinking powder," said Jake.

"I want to see if it works."

He shook some over Kipper.

Kipper began to shrink. "Help!"
he said. "Everything looks big."

"Hooray!" said Jake. "It works!"

"Oh no!" said Biff and Chip.

"Kipper has shrunk."

"It's not funny," said Kipper.

Jake tapped Kipper with a wand.

"Now I'll make him big," he said.

Suddenly, Kipper had huge ears.
"Whoops!" said Jake. "That's not
quite right ... let me try again."

Jake waved the wand. Suddenly, Kipper had long, green hair.

"This is *not* funny," said Kipper.

Jake waved the wand again.

"I *am* sorry," said Jake. "I can't make him big."

Chip was cross. He took Jake's
wand. "Let *me* try," he said.
Just then, the key glowed.

The key took them back. Kipper's big ears and green hair had gone, but he was still small.

"Dad is coming," said Chip. "We can't let him see Kipper."

"Let's put a box on him," said Biff.

Suddenly, Kipper was big again.
"What are you up to?" asked Dad.

"Shrinking Kipper," said Biff.
"That's a good joke!" laughed
Dad.

Think about the story

Jake's mistakes – rhyming pairs

Jake has put the wrong labels on the pictures.
Can you find the right ones?

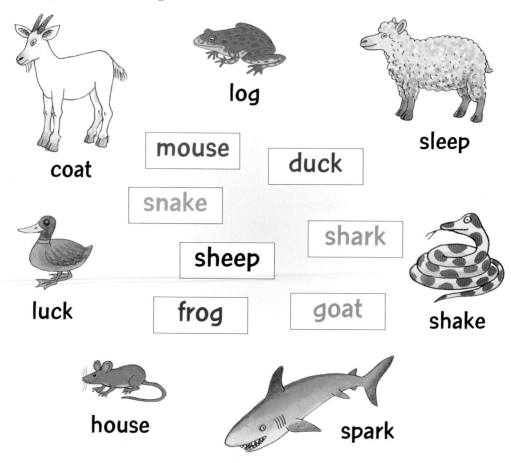

coat   log   sleep

mouse   duck

snake

sheep   shark

luck   frog   goat   shake

house   spark

**Useful common words repeated in this story and
other books in the series.**

boy   clothes   everything   funny   good   laughed   look
sorry   suddenly   that('s)   too   want   what('s)
Names in this story: Dad   Biff   Chip   Jake   Kipper

More books for you to enjoy

Level 1:
Getting Ready

Level 2:
Starting to Read

Level 3:
Becoming a Reader

Level 4:
Building Confidence

Level 5:
Reading with Confidence

OXFORD
UNIVERSITY PRESS

Great Clarendon Street,
Oxford OX2 6DP

Text © Roderick Hunt 2006
Illustrations © Alex Brychta 2006

First published 2006
All rights reserved

Series Editors: Kate Ruttle,
Annemarie Young

British Library Cataloguing
in Publication Data available

ISBN–13: 978-019-279235-8

10 9 8 7 6 5 4 3

Printed in China by Imago

Have more fun with Read at Home

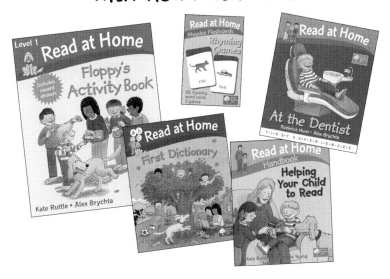